Vinnie Dra

Vinny Drake is One

Audrey Hopkins

Illustrated by Helen Flook

ANDERSEN PRESS
LONDON

First published in 2006 by
Andersen Press Limited,
20 Vauxhall Bridge Road, London SW1V 2SA
www.andersenpress.co.uk

British Library Cataloguing in Publication Data
available
ISBN-10: 1 84270 437 0
ISBN-13: 978 1 84270 437 0

Phototypeset by Intype Libra Ltd
Printed and bound in Great Britain by
Bookmarque Ltd., Croydon,
Surrey

Chapter 1

Vinny Drake *is* one. True!

He is too! He is one.

We know as soon as Miss Oddie fetches him in.

As soon as old Oddbody fetches him in we know. *I* just know and nobody has to tell us, tell *me* anything.

As soon as he's through the door and in our classroom and standing there as big as Miss Oddie but thinner, not fat, we cross our eyes, wrinkle our noses and nod because we know what he is.

Me and Daniel Stott nod and wrinkle our noses.

Vicky Parr winks and nudges Farley Haversham who winks back.

Vicky Parr can't cross her eyes and Farley Haversham's always look a bit funny without his glasses on.

We know what he is!

7

It's as plain as the big nose on B'n'B's face.

B'n'B's real name is Brian Barber but we call him B'n'B because his mum has got the bed and breakfast near the big church.

There's a sign there and I thought the church was called 'Bed and Breakfast' when I was four and stupid.

There's another sign next to it and that says 'The Parish Church of St Martin' so it's not a B'n'B.

But . . . it's as plain as the big, sticky-out nose on Brian Barber's face and he has a big one that anybody can see sticking out like a banana, if they've got eyes.

William Westerton's got eyes behind his glasses but he only looks at things in books.

Miss Oddie says he's a bookworm but he's just a worm, really.

Willie Westerton's a keen bean who reads books – big books – all the time and he knows everything that's in a book because he's always looking in one and reading everything.

That's why his eyes are a bit funny,
sort of squinty.

'They don't exist,' he says. 'They are
figments of the imagination. They are
legends thought up to have somebody
to blame when things go wrong.
Things like cows with three legs and
warts coming and things like that.
Things like mishaps. Witches are the
same . . . and goblins.'

Willie Westerton has three warts.

Willie Westerton is a nerd and talks like his dad.

Willie Westerton talks like a parrot that says everything somebody says when they've said it first. He says it second.

Mr Westerton looks
like a parrot. He
looks like a parrot
that's got a bit of
vulture in it.

Willie looks like
a smallish parrot, or
a budgie or an owl.
Mr Westerton is our
Head Teacher and
he's a grown-up nerd
as well as a vulture.

'What's a figment?' Farley says.

'A figment is a thing made up in your mind,' Willie says, pointing to his head – which is pointed.

Nerd!

'What sort of mishaps did they get blamed for, these figment things?' I ask him.

'I get blamed for everything in our house. Storms, floods, spilt milk and broken plates, birthmarks on . . .'

'Shut up, Daniel!'

'I've got a birthmark. What does that mean? Does it mean I'm a figment?'

'It means you're a geek, Farley Haversham, and Willie Westerton doesn't know everything in the world.

'Books tell lies, we all know that and we know what he is!'

We know . . . Daniel Stott, Farley Haversham, Vicky Parr and me.

We know all right!

We know a figment when we see one and this one's for real.

He's standing there with Miss Oddie and it's as plain as the nose on Big-nose Brian Barber's face, which is very plain because it's so big – but not as big as Mr Westerton's vulture beak.

First – he's very nice looking, like somebody in a boy band, somebody on the telly. He's nice looking, even handsome, but a bit thin and pale, also creepy.

Second – his eyes, like two black beads all glinty, are sunk in and sort of sneaky and his hair is black. His hair is very shiny like it's painted on and it comes to a point at the front.

Third – he's got fangs. He's got biting teeth that show when he talks

and when he grins, like he's doing
right there next to Miss Oddie – just
standing there and grinning with his
fangs showing and Oddbody's not even
noticed.

We have noticed.

Fangs! He's got two of them that are too big for his mouth. Two very big and pointy fangs that make dents in his bottom lip.

HIS VERY RED BOTTOM LIP. BLOOD RED!

Who else is very pale and very thin?

Who else has shiny black hair that comes to a point?

Who else has pointy fangs except DRRR-AAA-CU-LAA?

Aaarrgh!

He's tall as well. He's as tall as Miss Oddbody-Oddie is but he's a lot thinner and nearly as tall as Mr Vulture-Westerton is and he's wearing a shiny black anorak, not a cape. (The

new boy is wearing the anorak, not Mr Westerton, who always wears grey).

A shiny black anorak with a black zip, also shiny.

Creepy!

Chapter 2

'This is Vincent Drake,' Miss Oddie is telling us when we've stopped holding our breaths and rolling our crossed eyes (and Willie his squinty ones) at each other.

We have also stopped wrinkling our noses and nodding in case he spots us at it.

'He has come to live in our village,' Miss Oddie says.

Our village?

He has come to live in our village where everybody knows everybody and everybody is nice and doesn't have shiny black hair and pointy fangs?

Why has he come to our village with his fangs and black anorak?

Did anybody ask us if we wanted a figment in our village . . . a figment that makes mishaps?

There are clues, plenty of them!

1. 'Vincent'! That's a real vampire's name, I've seen one on a video. Vincent Price was his name and he was a vampire. I've seen one called Christopher as well but not on the same video.

2. 'Drake!' That's short for Dracula because he couldn't go around using his real name. He couldn't come to our school calling himself Vincent Dracula, could he? Would he?

What . . . How . . . Yaargh!

'There's b-b-blood on his sh-sh-shirt,' I gasp, clutching my throat in case he fancies it.

'Tomato sauce I think,' know-all Willie Westerton says.

'Get lost, Westerton. Quit thinking so much, you'll hurt your brain,' I tell him. 'It's blood!'

'So . . . who is going to look after Vincent today?' Miss Oddie says, pressing her fingertips together and smiling at us.

Smiling makes her look young and pretty – she thinks.

Pretty horrible – I think!

Silence. Gulp, gulp.

'Not me,' whispered at the back.

I'm the bravest so who's afraid of a figment – or even a big bad wolf – not me!

'Me,' I say with my hand up. 'I'll look after him.'

It's very brave of me, saving the others from his biting fangs and they'll have to pay me back lots.

Besides, he's a bit nice, sort of. He's a bit nice – if creepy.

'Hello, Vincent, I'm Flora,' I tell him.

'Call me Vinny,' he says.

'Don't you dare call me Flo!' I warn him and he grins.

When he grins his fangs show a lot, very long and sharp. I rub my neck but I won't scream.

'I won't then,' he says, still grinning.

Won't what . . . bite my neck? He's reading my brain, grinning and watching me rubbing my neck and his eyes are sort of shiny and black with diamonds in them – but that might be the lights.

'Won't what?' I ask him.

'Won't call you Flo,' he says. 'Flora's much nicer, sort of flowery.'

Vinny Drake is a vampire but I like him.

'When did you first know you are one?' I ask him when Miss Oddie has her head in the cupboard.

'One what?' he says.

'You know. One of the undead.'

His eyebrows meet in the middle and he looks a bit fierce now he's stopped grinning. What if he does bite my neck, will I be one too?

'I don't know what you're on about,' he says.

He's not very bright, for an undead.

'A vampire. A Dracula. You are one, Vinny, we can tell. Were you born like it or did he bite you?'

'Who?'

'Him, the chief vampire. Whose blood is that?'

He squints at his shirt. 'It's ketchup!'

'Don't lie, Vinny, it's not honest. When did you last have a bite?'

'This morning. I had a fried egg sandwich with tomato sauce on it.'

He won't admit it, will he?

Poor Vincent. He doesn't even know what vampires do.

Vinny the Vamp needs help and I'm Flora the Fearless. I'll help him. I'll train him to be the best one there is – round here anyway.

Chapter 3

There are plans to make and lessons to learn.

Miss Oddie agrees about that so we do arithmetic. Some of us do arithmetic because we're swots and do everything Oddbody says whether we like it or not.

Some of us do it when it's mental arithmetic because she's got her eyes on us and we have to or she shouts.

Some of us, like me, make notes in our rough books when she's writing on the blackboard.

The next class up has a white board with black pen things but ours is the chalky sort . . . very dusty.

Miss Oddie always says she has eyes in the back of her head but it isn't true because I've done tests to prove it – like pulling faces and getting up and stretching but she never sees me, never knows.

She is lying about her extra eyes.

I make notes in my rough book and she'll never know because rough books are ours alone and private.

Vicky Carr draws doodles in hers and sometimes scribbles out things like Vicky 4 Daniel and Danny 4ever so nobody can see she likes him a lot but I know she does.

I used to like him too, till Vinny.

So, I make important notes in my rough book using red crayon to underline the very important bits.

Vampires usually sleep all day, get up at sunset and stay out all night biting people for blood.

Vinny's mum and dad wouldn't like him to do that, unless they are vampires too and know what to do.

'Do you look like your mum and dad, Vinny?'

He doesn't.

Vinny's mum is little and quite fat and his dad is a milkman, also little and fatter and he gets UP at dawn instead of going to sleep in his personal coffin.

Vampires have their own wooden coffins with their own private dirt in it, special dirt that's been dug up in their own land.

Vinny isn't quite that sort of vampire.

He can't stay out all night because his mum and dad would go mad and

start calling the police and he hasn't got a dirt coffin so we'll have to forget about that and do everything in the daytime.

Which is just a bit annoying.

Ouch! A little blob of blood squeezes out of the pinhole in my thumb.

I made the pinhole with a safety pin, for safety.

'Did it hurt?' Vinny asks.

'I'm not doing that for anybody,' Vicky says with her hands in her pockets in case I grab a thumb and stick the pin in her before she can say Jack Robinson. (That's what Dad says when he means 'right now' but I don't know Mr Robinson.)

'I'm not!' Vicky says again.

Who asked her to?

'Go on, Vinny, drink it,' I order, squeezing harder.

First he won't and then he does and pulls a face.

'Yuck!' he says. 'No way, Flora, you taste horrible.'

'I thought Dracula was supposed to be charming,' I tell him.

'I'm not . . .'

'Forget it!'

So, he can't stay out all night and he doesn't like the taste of blood – not even *my* blood!

Some vampire!

Chapter 4

Flying is easy-peasy lemon squeezy.

Vinny isn't so sure.

'How can a human fly?' he says,
trying to get away and moaning a lot.

'You are not human, Vinny Drake,
hold still and be told!'

Vicky has a garage. It's right at the
bottom of her garden near a big tree
and behind that tree is the garden wall
and over the garden wall is the alley.

We go down the alley and climb the
wall to get into the garden.

Easy-peasy!

Vicky's garage roof is very useful . . . also flat.

It has been a boat, a desert island, the 'Star Ship Enterprise' and the lost world in the middle of the jungle with dinosaurs in it.

Farley saw a video about that.

'I can't fly!' Vinny shouts from the garage roof.

'Shut up and tie the rope!'

'He's forgotten how to do it,' Vicky says. 'He's lost his memory on the long and dangerous journey from Transilwotsit, Draculaland.'

'We came from Sheffield,' Vinny says, moaning and wriggling.

Draculas *should* moan but only at night to scare people.

'Only from Sheffield,' he moans.

'Sheffield in Yorkshire or Sheffield in Transylvania – it makes no difference. You can't kid us, Vinny Drake.'

He's on the edge of the garage roof and he is shivering and shaking. His knees are knocking and his teeth are chattering.

He's on the edge of the roof with a clothesline tied round his middle and it's padded with his jumper so it won't dig in his ribs and hurt him.

It would be better if he was fatter but he isn't so he's padded with his jumper.

I, Flora Gould, think of everything.

One day I'll be a teacher.

The clothesline is round Vinny's middle and the other end is up the tree with Daniel Stott.

Daniel is tying the rope round the tree in case Vinny can't fly.

Vinny can't!

He's swinging there, back and round and round with the rope under his armpits and his toes kicking the dandelions.

Vinny says it hurts in a very squeaky voice and his pale face is paler – nearly white. He's kicking himself off the garage wall with his muddy trainers and he's making footprints on the white paint.

That'll make people think. Nobody can walk up walls except Spiderman . . . and Vinny Drake who is a vampire.

'Flap you arms, Vinny. Flap. Flap. Fly!'

Vinny flaps.

He flops . . . The rope broke!

41

Chapter 5

Easy-peasy lemon squeezy . . . Vinny
Drake isn't very happy because of the
bruises round his middle.

He wouldn't have got any bruises if
he'd done it right, if he'd been a proper
bat, a vampire bat.

'What do bats do besides fly about,
Flora?' he says.

'Don't ask *her*, she's never seen one.'

'Who says I haven't, Farley Haversham?'

'Me!'

'Have you, then, know-all?' I ask him.

'Too right. I've seen them tons of times on the telly,' he says. 'They hang upside down in bat caves, bats do, and they fly out at night to hunt blood.'

Vinny is not happy.

'I'm not going in a bat cave. It'll be dark and smelly and I know I can't fly out. We *all* know I can't fly out.'

'Forget the flying bit,' I tell him. 'You like the dark, Vinny. All vampires do.'

'I'm not going in any cave!'

'Who says you have to? Wait till dinnertime.'

'I'm not messing in any cave. I'll miss dinner and I've paid for it.'

Vinny Drake is a dork. Only dorks eat school dinners. Proper people spend their dinner money on crisps and cheesy bites.

At dinnertime Daniel Stott clears the cloakroom.

'Out!' he says and everybody 'outs'.

'This is a cloakroom,' Vinny says.

'This is a cave, Vinny. It is a bat cave in disguise.'

'This is a cloakroom. It's got coats on pegs and shoes in the lockers. It is a cloakroom, Flora.'

'It is a bat cave, Vinny, believe it.'

If Vinny does a handstand on the lockers we can fasten his feet to the pegs, can't we? That should remind him of home – his bat cave in Sheffield.

'It isn't safe. It's all moving and shaking,' Vinny moans.

He does a lot of moaning does Vinny Drake.

'It won't break, Vinny, honest,' we tell him when we have him upside down. 'We've swung on them lots of times and they haven't broken.'

We take off his shoes and turn him

upside down then we fasten him up
with school ties. We tie them round his
feet and we let him keep his socks on.
Farley holds him up till he's done.

'OK, Vamp, hang cool!'

Vinny says it hurts.

He's upside down and we can see
right up his nose. His eyes look funny
the wrong way up. He looks a bit
cross-eyed.

His eyebrows look like a moustache and his pointy hair looks a bit like a beard. His ears look the same as always.

Upside down though.

'Ow, ouch,' he moans.

'Practise for a bit, Vinny. You have to practise. Practice makes perfect my mum says when I'm scraping my viola. You sound a bit like my viola when I'm playing it, Vinny. Sort of scrapy and screechy and horrible. It sounds quite good when Mr Ford plays it. Funny, that.'

Vinny's blood is running down into his head. He says he can't feel his feet but he has a headache.

I think he's looking much better already – more pink and more like a human.

That's what he needed you see – more blood in his head.

That's why they have to bite necks and drink it, the undead.

The bell goes and we can't unfasten our school ties.

We'll be in trouble if we're not wearing our ties.

We'll be sent to Mr Westerton and shouted at if we're not wearing our ties.

Ties must be worn at all times.

'Hang on, Vinny, hang cool till the end of school.'

Vinny's wearing his tie so he won't get shouted at. (Not for that, anyway.)

Watch it, Flora, the vulture's coming!

Spoilsport!

Mr Westerton unties Vinny and Oddbody gives him a hug . . .

Gross!

We just get shouted at but who wants a teacher hug anyway?

Chapter 6

Grounded!

Flora Gould is grounded at home and kept inside at playtime like a criminal.

Helping Vinny Drake to be a good vampire is not criminal, is it?

I wish I hadn't bothered.

Vinny Drake is a grasser, a tell tale.

He grasses to Miss Oddie.

He grasses to Vicky Parr's dad about the footprints up the garage wall and he grasses to Willie Westerton's dad, the vulture.

Vinny Drake tells tales.

Vincent Leon Adrian Drake is not a vampire, even if his initials do spell VLAD!

Vlad the Impaler stuck his enemies on spikes, just for fun. The picture's in a book. Yuck!

'Bullying will not be tolerated in this school, Flora Gould,' Vulture Westerton said.

'Bullies are the lowest of the low,' old Oddbody said.

I am not a bully, a lowest of the low. I was helping.

Vinny Drake never was a vampire.

He fell off his bike and knocked his front teeth out, except for the pointy ones, the fangs.

He's pale because he was sick with something; he doesn't know its name but it was horrible being in bed all the time.

Miss Oddie says that bullies are the lowest of the low but that isn't true.

Snakes are.

Grasser . . . Grass snake . . . Drake the Snake, Drake the fake, cornflake, go jump in the lake and see if I care.

Vinny Drake is a grasser and a greaser but . . .

'Be my friend to the end,' he says. 'The queen of my scene, my bite for tonight.'

Fun-ny! Vinny's funny. Vinny's ace.

'Where have the fangs gone, Vinny?'

'Gone to Mrs Ruth the tooth and her electric torture chair.'

'Where's the hair?'

'Cropped. Short back and topped.'

New hair curling, new teeth coming, no more Vinny the Vamp.

He's nice, is Vincent Drake.

Vincent Drake likes Flora Gould . . . True.

Vinny 4 Flora + Flora 4 Vinny.

I let him bite my neck, just a bit and it doesn't hurt at all, just tickles.

Miss Oddie is coming in and she's fetching a new . . .

Hold it! It sticks out a mile.

It's as plain as the nose on Big-nose Brian Barber's face.

First – He's big and wide.

Second – There are stitches near his eyebrows.

Third – His head looks square with that haircut, sort of flat on top and why has he got that scarf round his neck?

What, exactly, is he hiding under that scarf?

A lump?

A vampire bite?

A nut and bolt?

Who else?

It sticks out a mile!

He moves . . . he clinks . . . he jangles . . . WHO ELSE?

'Hold my hand, Vinny.'

'Quiet! Miss Oddie's talking –
listen.'

'We have another new boy today.
This is Frank.'

Frank who?

'Frank En . . .'

Eeeek . . . aarrgh . . . aarroogh!